For my mother and father M.D.

Author's Note:

In 1923, a few months before his death, the author Franz Kafka met a little girl who was crying because she had lost her doll. To comfort her, Kafka suggested that the doll had gone away, but promised to write, and himself sent letters describing the doll's travels. The incident inspired this story.

HAMISH HAMILTON LTD

Published by the Penguin Group
27 Wrights Lane, London W8 5TZ, England
Penguin Books USA Inc, 375 Hudson Street, New York, New York 10014, USA
Penguin Books Australia Ltd, Ringwood, Victoria, Australia
Penguin Books Canada Ltd, 10 Alcorn Avenue, Toronto, Ontario, Canada M4V 3B2
Penguin Books (NZ) Ltd, 182-190 Wairau Road, Auckland 10, New Zealand

Penguin Books Ltd, Registered Offices: Harmondsworth, Middlesex, England

First published in Great Britain 1993 by Hamish Hamilton Ltd

Text copyright © 1993 by Jean Richardson
Illustrations copyright © 1993 by Mike Dodd

1 3 5 7 9 10 8 6 4 2

The moral rights of the author and artist have been asserted

Mike Dodd is represented by the Maggie Mundy Illustrators' Agency

The full colour illustrations were done with Schwan Stabilo Softcolor pencils and Rexel Derwent Studio
pencils on sand-coloured Ingres paper. The small sepia illustrations were done with Berol Karisma
Graphite Aquarelle pencils, Rexel Derwent Studio pencils and Winsor & Newton gouache wash
on 90lb watercolour paper.

British Library Cataloguing in Publication Data
CIP data for this book is available from the British Library

ISBN 0-241-13357-2

Printed in Italy by L.E.G.O.

THE · LOST · DOLL

Pictures by
MIKE · DODD

Story by
JEAN · RICHARDSON

HAMISH HAMILTON · LONDON

Harriet knew she shouldn't disturb her father when
he was busy, but what she had to say couldn't wait.

"Daddy! Daddy! Something awful's
happened. I've lost Lottie." And because it
was so awful and she was so upset, Harriet burst
into tears.

The two men looked surprised. The visitor,
whose name was Mr Kafka and whom Harriet
liked at once, offered her an enormous
handkerchief to mop up her tears.

"Not now, Harriet," her father said gently.
"I'm busy. Tell me all about it later on."

But Mr Kafka wanted to know who Lottie was. "Is she a dog, a cat, a mouse, an elephant...?"

Harriet couldn't help smiling at his question, and that at once made her feel a little better. Lottie, she explained, was a doll. "I took her for a walk in the park and somehow, I don't know how, she got lost."

"She may not be lost," Mr Kafka said gravely. "I once met a doll who had to go away, but she promised to write to her Mama. I wouldn't be surprised if you got a letter from Lottie."

Harriet found this hard to believe. She wasn't very good at writing letters, and neither, she was sure, was Lottie.

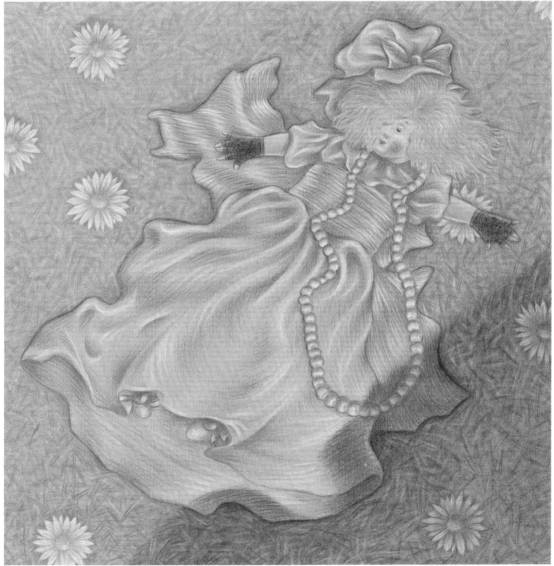

Her father told her later that Mr Kafka was a very famous author. He was ill, and he was going on a long holiday to make him better.

Harriet, who liked the way Mr Kafka had realised that Lottie was a real person, hoped that he would get well.

She looked for Lottie every time they
went to the park. Under bushes.
In litter bins: a dreadful thought!
Even in the lake, just in case Lottie
had fallen in and been washed ashore.
But there was no sign of the lost doll.

Tuesday 25th March 1923

Dearest Mama
Please don't be X with me! And don't worry
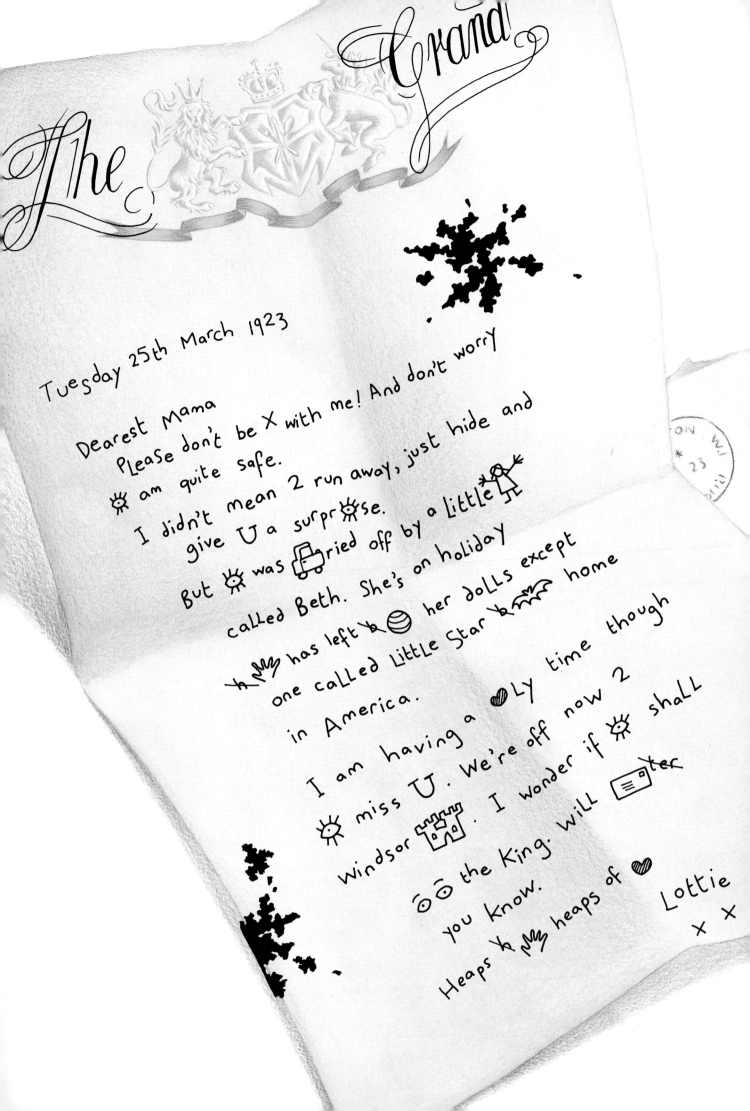 am quite safe.
I didn't mean 2 run away, just hide and
give U a surpr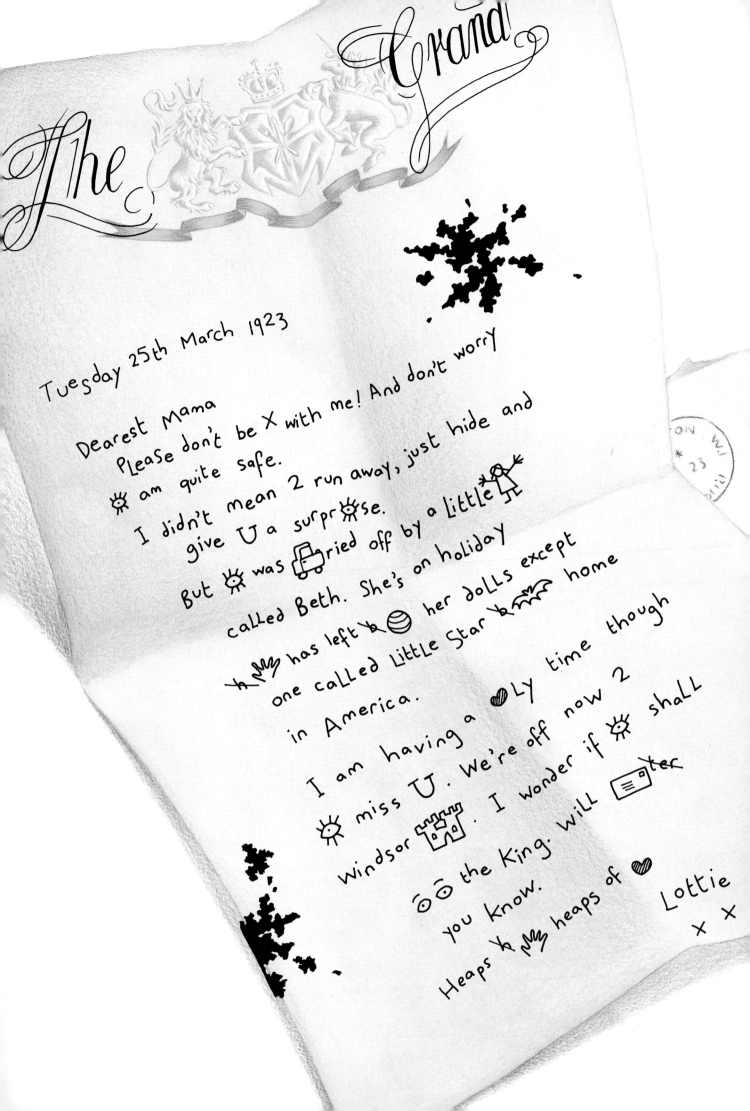se.
But 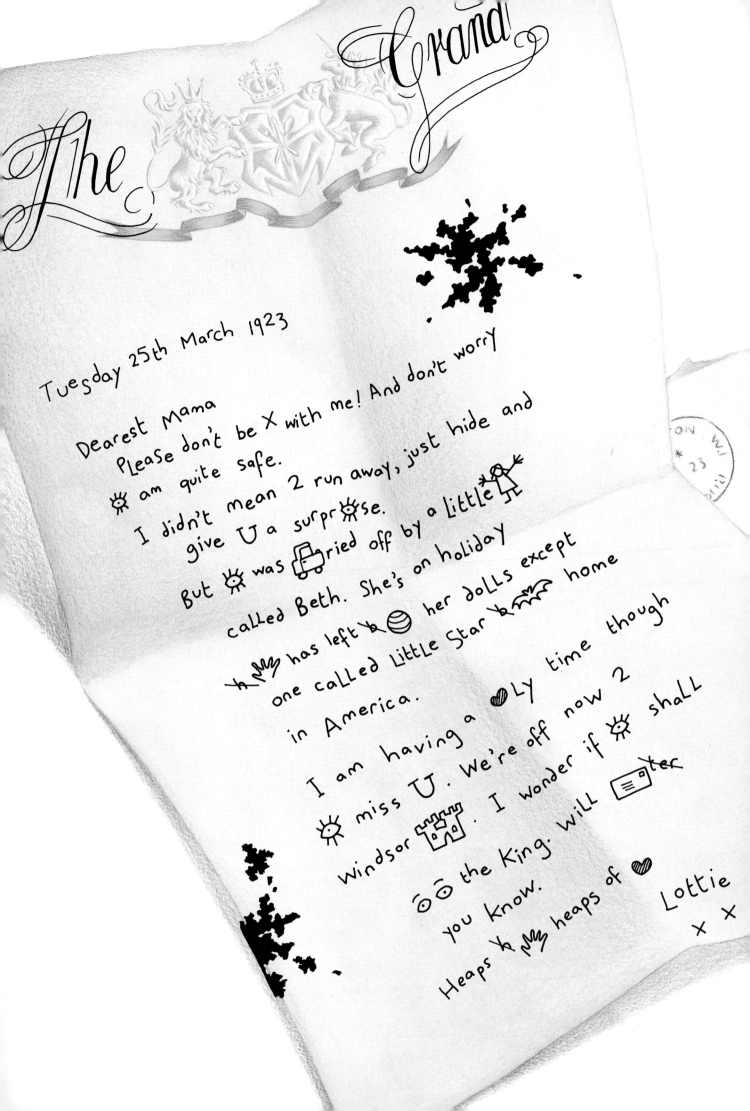 was 🚗rried off by a Little
🖐 has left 🎈 her dolls except
one called Little Star 🦇 home
called Beth. She's on holiday
in America.
I am having a 🖤ly time though
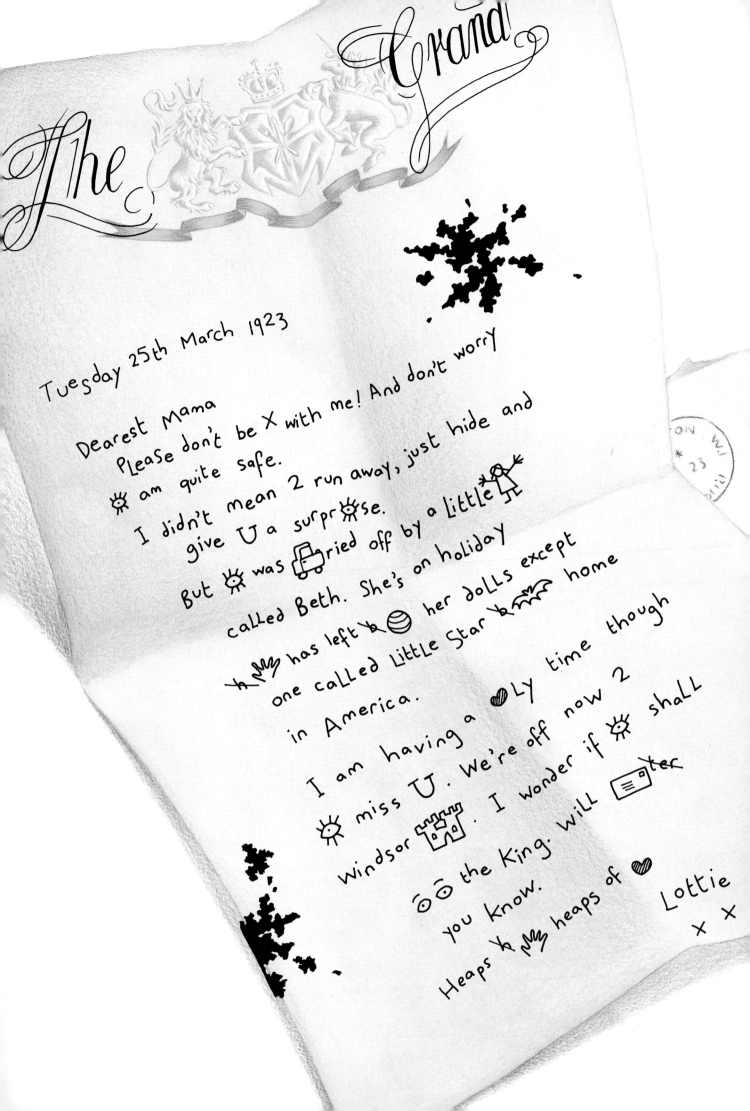 miss U. We're off now 2
Windsor 🏰. I wonder if 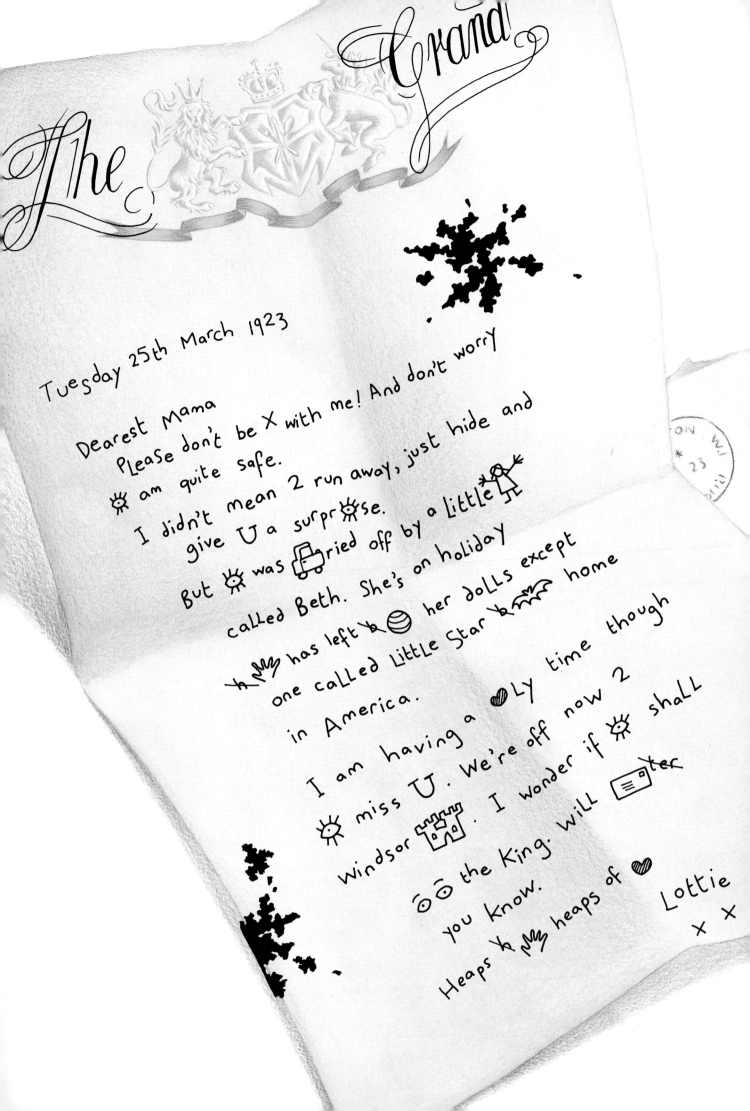 shall
👀 the King. Will ✉️ter
you know.
Heaps 🖐 heaps of 🖤

Lottie
x x

Then, a week later, when Harriet had given up hope, she got a most unexpected letter.

It was written in dolls' writing, with pictures sometimes instead of words. The address at the top was that of a famous hotel, and the envelope was postmarked London, W1.

Harriet was delighted that Lottie wasn't lost - but she was cross with her. It didn't seem fair that after being so naughty, she should be having such a good time.

She decided to sort out her dolls' wardrobe, and when she saw Lottie's clothes, they made her feel sad all over again.

Harriet was glad that when Lottie disappeared,
she had been wearing one of her prettiest dresses
and her favourite necklace.

At least her new mother – what a dreadful idea!
– would see she had been well looked after.

She was wondering whether to send a parcel
of Lottie's warmer clothes to the hotel, when a
postcard arrived.

Dear Mama

👁 Wish U could 👀 me.

Beth has bought me some new clothes 🌸🌸 Little Star says ☀ Look very 🌟k!

I am very proud of my new 👒 which has a curly 🪶 in it.

Au Revoir   Lottie ✗✗

Miss Harriet West
5 Eastbourne Terrace
London W2

ANGLETERRE

✗ ✗ ✗ ✗

Harriet only just rescued the postcard in time, as her brother was trying to steam off the French stamp. When she saw the picture of the Eiffel Tower, her heart sank. Lottie, it seemed, was now in Paris and it had plainly gone to her head!

The next letter, from Venice, was full of woe.
Lottie had fallen out of a gondola – and she was
sure that Little Star had pushed her.

"Beth was showing us the Grand Canal when suddenly I found myself in it. Luckily I was rescued, but I caught a cold from being dumped in a carrier bag in wet clothes – and that was the last I saw of Venice."

Harriet felt very worried about Lottie. Beth wouldn't know she had a weak chest and needed to wear her flannel petticoat when she had a cold.

158   EGYPTIAN TYPES AND SCENES – The Market

But Lottie had travelled south, into the sun.

    "Today Little Star saved my life," she wrote
dramatically on the back of a postcard of a
colourful street market.

"A mountain of fruit tumbled off one of the stalls. Little Star saw it and pushed us out of the way – just in time. We might all have been buried under oranges, lemons, pineapples and figs. Little Star is now my very best friend."

Lottie was really travelling. She wrote from stations, trains, hotels and pavement cafés. And once from the back of an elephant. She didn't have time to write much. Sometimes only "Hi! We're here!"

Just before Christmas, Harriet received a letter
and a parcel. It was about the right size for a doll,
and Harriet's heart beat faster at the thought that
it might, at long last, be Lottie come home.

Although she longed to see Lottie, Harriet
was afraid to open the parcel, so she read the
letter first. It was written on board a
famous liner.

When she had read the letter, Harriet wept. She
knew, deep down, that there wouldn't be any
more letters.

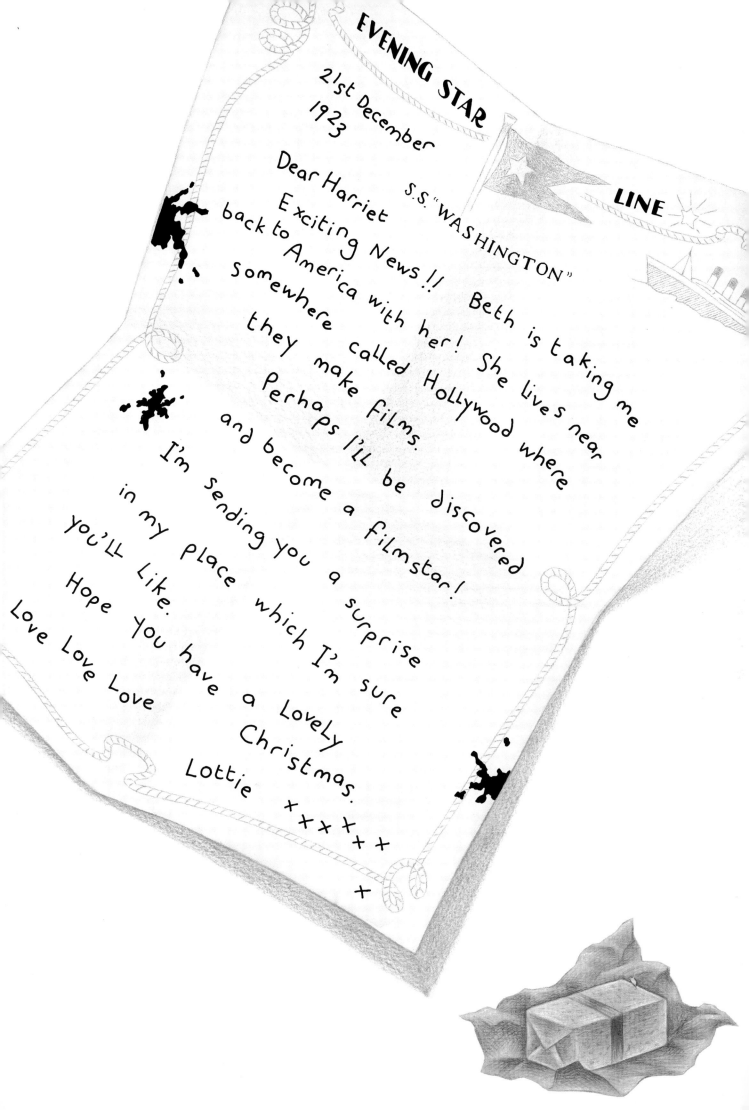

EVENING STAR

LINE

21st December
1923

S.S. "WASHINGTON"

Dear Harriet

Exciting News !!   Beth is taking me
back to America with her! She lives near
somewhere called Hollywood where
they make films.
Perhaps I'll be discovered
and become a filmstar!

I'm sending you a surprise
in my place which I'm sure
you'll Like.
Hope you have a Lovely
Love Love Love Christmas.
Lottie ✕ ✕ ✕ ✕ ✕

✕

She didn't hurry to undo the parcel that
didn't, after all, contain Lottie.

But when at last she did, she found
herself looking at a very tired and frightened
doll. Harriet had no doubt who she was, for
pinned to her dress was a little brooch with
the name LITTLE STAR.

Harriet gave Little Star a big comforting hug.
"How brave of you to travel right across the world
all by yourself," she said.

Then she tucked Little Star under the
coverlet in Lottie's pram. "You must be very tired.
No talking tonight. You can tell me all your news
in the morning."

Little Star shut her eyes obediently. She had
long dark plaits and was very pretty in her own
way - though it wasn't Lottie's way.

Harriet would like to have told
Mr Kafka that he was right about
Lottie's adventures, but he was gone.
Just as now Lottie was gone, too.

As Little Star was the same size as Lottie, all Lottie's clothes fitted her and Harriet kept her American clothes for best.

They often went to the park. Little Star liked to hear the story of how Lottie had disappeared, though Harriet was careful never to give her the chance to run away and hide.

But Little Star, who loved Harriet dearly, had had quite enough adventures for any doll.